# Analekta

an anthology of writing

Analekta – Volume 1

Copyright © 2012

All rights to this anthology are reserved. No part of this book may be reproduced in any form or by any electronic or mechanical means, including information storage and retrieval systems, without written permission from the authors or publisher.

Rights to the individual works contained in this anthology are owned by the submitting authors and each has permitted the work's use in this collection.

ISBN: 978-0-9891181-0-1

eISBN: 978-0-9891181-1-8

Printed in the United States of America

Boho Books edition/May 2013

# Contents

Introduction

| | | |
|---|---|---|
| K. D. Schmidt | 3 | Last Day |
| | 38 | Untitled Poem |
| Pattie PalmerBaker | 5 | The Poem, Waiting |
| | 39 | Grieving Mallards |
| | 48 | Advice For The Artist's Husband |
| Larry Anderson | 6 | Perspective |
| | 14 | Another Rainy Commute |
| Dani Clifton | 7 | Sins Of A Father |
| Lizzy Welle OeDell | 16 | Tiny Mr. Spider |
| | 47 | Lake |
| Carrol Haushalter | 17 | The Year Chickens Wore Underpants |
| Glen Bledsoe | 19 | Forever & Eternity |
| John Sibley Williams | 29 | The Castle |
| Devon Seale | 41 | Through Sun Or Storm |
| Angie Hughes | 49 | Jamie G. Has Changed |

Contributors
Our Thanks
Submission Guidelines

## Introduction

The Pacific Northwest has proved a fertile ground for growing literary centers. Cities such as Portland, Seattle, and San Francisco are beacons to those who wish to make their literal mark on the world of writing and publishing. Beyond the urban, however, other writers also dream and write down those dreams on tables located in small communities or set in rural landscapes.

The co-founders of *Analekta* know these writers because this is also where we live. We have read these writers' words, listened to their hopes, and offered them our encouragement. Out of their dreams, we've realized one of our own: creating an anthology that draws attention to the talent hidden among the fields and barns, tucked into tiny towns, and located off the beaten paths.

Analekta simply means "selected things". This anthology presents selections of written works that showcase the talented wordsmiths of Oregon's Clackamas, Marion, Multnomah, and Washington counties. Its purpose—other than to satisfy the many appetites of readers from all walks of life—is to discover and nurture writers, giving attention to those who choose to work within the techniques and conventions of both genre writing and poetry, and to serve as a portal to the countless worlds that words afford.

Happy reading!

—L. Lee Shaw & Heather Frazier, Analekta Editors

# Last Day
## K. D. Schmidt

SHE APPROACHED THE ENTRANCE OF the hospice room quietly, though it wouldn't have made a difference—the coma induced by the medications rendered the woman in the bed oblivious.

The early light of that sunny July morning was filtered by a long curtain of yellow chiffon. The nurse, having issue about color coordination, had changed the bed linens, and gently bathed and dressed the grandmother in a nightgown so that all matched the buttery hue—giving her and the entire room a golden, ethereal glow. It had been only six weeks from diagnosis to this time and place. Not enough time to prepare mentally, emotionally, spiritually.

The priest arrived the day before, gathering the family, anointing her with an essence of Frankincense, and reciting the prayers that accompanied the centuries-old sacrament of extreme unction. Tears rolled down familiar faces as he pronounced Jeanette Elizabeth as being in a state of grace and ready to safely traverse this world to the next.

It had turned to the present, and the room had only two occupants, an elderly woman of enduring beauty, and the granddaughter who loved her beyond reason. The younger woman was faced with one of the most timeless of all dilemmas: how to say the final goodbye.

In earnest, how does one say farewell to the woman who saved her life repeatedly, nursed her to health—repeatedly, encouraged in her an intense curiosity in all matters, and infused her with a love for learning? What is the regular order of things when your kindred soul is about to join the spiritual realm exclusively?

The bed-fast female slumbered easily—unlike the previous days, when it was obvious an internal struggle ensued, accompanied by restlessness and even a short period of consciousness and impressive lucidity. Now, to say the elaborate words of love and gratitude the granddaughter longed to have her grandmother hear would be impractical, at the least.

After much deliberation, she went with something visceral. Moving to her grandmother's bedside, she paused over the sleeping form and took a deep breath through her nostrils, taking in the sweet scent of her, trying to file it away in the most primitive portion of the brain for remembrance. She then gently shifted the legs so that she could comfortably sit and lie down next to her one last time, and taking that beautiful, peaceful face in her hands, she kissed it repeatedly, slowly, softly—starting with the chin, moving to each cheek, the tip of the nose, and finally finishing with a tender, lingering kiss on the forehead. With each kiss she uttered two phrases sequentially: "Thank you" and "I love you".

The granddaughter maintained that position for the better part of an hour, delicately brushing the hair out of her grandmother's face with her fingers, marveling at the high cheekbones, strong jaw line, and skin surprisingly unlined for the eighty-three years of life that existed beneath it. More importantly, revering the courage, character, and, most of all, the compassion that emanated beyond the face and form.

A sound beyond the room indicated that her ride to her home in the North was ready and waiting. The young woman carefully removed herself from the bed, gained her footing and turned to look at the woman in the bed a final time. Staring as though to imprint the image, she would access it in easy recall in the years to come: her beloved—serene and radiant.

## The Poem, Waiting
Pattie PalmerBaker

The next poem I write will cut close to the bone—
no not just close, this poem will be my spine
a stem winding through my center
pushing up my red-rose heart
no not a rose, a bud clenched green
as the stem reposed in pain.

In my next poem I lie next to you
and say I want to know
what it is like to be you
to be inside of you
for a moment
for thirty seconds.

You say to me
I am inside of you
I live there.

This is the poem I want to write,
for you I open my body every orifice.
I am a sun-orange tulip the petals unfold
and there black feather-centered
a yellow star glows.

## Perspective
Larry Anderson

I look down railroad tracks—and see
a slow coming together
of all problems. Clarity will
walk with us—to the endpoint
at infinite joy and reconciliation.

The tracks are steel hard
buttressed by decaying matter—
smelling of futile attempts
to sanctify the present.

I keep walking—expecting
narrowing. Nothing changes—
the poor—stay poor. Hate
and anger—stay hate and
anger.

We wait to see the end.
I peer out, on my toes
and look for Jesus.
Nothing.

I look back. We missed him.

# Sins Of A Father
Dani Clifton

The monsters were real.

Lilliana Renfield stood at the window, looking out into the fog-filled night. She pulled the blanket closer to her shoulders and put on a brave front.

*Let me in.*

The cold fingers of foreboding ran themselves down her spine. She fingered the ruby pendant at her throat, a gift from her late father. From his hospice bed, in his last lucid moment, her father had pressed the talisman into her hand and whispered a cryptic message:

"The command of the necromancer is now yours. The Master's power is mighty, but the power inside of you is greater."

Those were the last words he ever spoke, to her or anyone. She hoped he'd spent his last moments in relative peace, his inner torment laid to rest.

*You cannot deny me, Lilliana. Let me in.*

Lilliana turned from the window and returned to her bed.

Rush hour traffic had finally extracted its claws from the city when RedCrow found herself on the seedier side of town and in one hell of a predicament: a wraith stood between her and the lonely alley's only exit. RedCrow hadn't been looking for trouble, but that didn't mean a damn thing; trouble had a habit of dogging her. The custom-made blade in RedCrow's grasp—forged for her hand alone—gave a false sense of hope that she might escape. A potent paralyzer, fear can also be a mighty motivator. Luckily, this wasn't RedCrow's first rodeo.

The wraith had started tailing her six blocks ago when she'd left the Diablo, a bar she worked at near an empty lot under the Fremont Bridge. Drawn to both her sacred spirit and warm flesh, it had been easy enough to lure the creature into the alley. It took a halting step forward swaying on its feet, making it appear clumsy and lethargic, but RedCrow wasn't fooled. Animated by dark magic and corruption, wraiths were wicked-fast and deadly; one touch of their flesh to hers and she would be one of them.

With sickening recognition, RedCrow realized the evil monstrosity before her had once been Father Ed from St. Ignatius parish down near the waterfront. Father Ed was a local hero among the city's poor, feeding the hungry and making sure those who sought refuge from the cold always had a warm place to sleep. All that Father Ed had been was no more. A shell of his former self, his human body was nothing more than a meat puppet now. Thin arms protruded from the sleeves of a tattered cassock; the white square at his collar was askew and stained. The priest's grey fingers scrabbled outward, catching the front of RedCrow's jacket with its dirty, brittle nails. She dodged full contact just in time and was able to put several yards between them.

Responding only to its need to feed, the wraith pushed forward, coming at RedCrow with preternatural speed. She was ready to land the fatal blow—a knife to the heart—when the wraith exhibited something akin to strategy, feigning right then dodging left when RedCrow altered her stance. She realized too late that her trajectory was all wrong and, at the last second, opted to slash out horizontally rather than go for the kill shot. The razor-sharp blade cut a neat line across the wraith's throat, nearly severing its head from its shoulders. The damage had no apparent effect. RedCrow altered her position for a second blow, this time plunging the knife into the creature's chest, delivering a final, true-death blow. Its unnatural life force abruptly severed by RedCrow's blade, the wraith's body crumpled, gravity sliding it off the blade with a slick, sucking sound.

The heavens opened and rain began to fall in earnest. RedCrow held her hands out before her and watched the fat drops fall onto her palms and run in black rivulets off her fingers. She wished the rain could wash her soul as easily.

Silent strobes of red and blue suddenly stabbed into the alley, illuminating RedCrow and the mess at her feet. There was no use trying to run. The first patrol car on the scene spit out a single screaming cop, red-faced and firearm drawn. RedCrow laced her fingers on top of her head and waited for the rest of the goon squad to arrive.

Lilliana Renfield was assailing the sandbag at the boxing club near her Pearl District loft when the call came in. She didn't stop to answer it, but instead ramped up her attack on the canvas bag as if it were personally responsible for the nightmares that fueled her insomnia. The cell phone quieted, only to begin ringing again seconds later. She scooped it up from the floor and breathed her name with impatience, "Renfield."

Twenty minutes later, her blue BMW pulled to the curb behind a line of police cruisers near the mouth of an alley. The air was thick with both the smell of diesel coming up from the docks beyond the buildings and the unmistakably sweet stench of death. Renfield pulled on a blue windbreaker and dropped a lanyard over her head from which dangled her official FBI identification. She made a quick visual sweep of the area before ducking under a strip of yellow crime scene tape.

Concentrated spotlights lit up the alley and the rotating blue-red lights atop the police cruisers reflected on every wet surface. Renfield recognized the man bent over the remains as Dr. Hedges, formerly of the county medical examiner's office, presently with the resurrected Majestic 12.

"Evening, Hedgehog," Renfield said as she neared the body. "Do you have time or cause of death yet?"

"Negative on both." Dr. Hedges stood and scratched the sandy scruff at his chin, "I don't get it—a body in this condition should be a forensic entomologist's *wet dream* but there's *zero* insect activity on these remains. I don't have so much as a single blow fly larva. It makes no sense." Dr. Hedges looked sheepishly at Renfield. "I was sort of hoping you might be able to pull a little of your necromancer mojo—"

Renfield shot the doctor a withering look.

"Do I look like a party favor to you?" she asked more severely than she meant to.

He hadn't really been out of line with his request, Renfield just needed to work on her patience. As the great-great-granddaughter of RM Renfield, plaything, servant, and occasional snack to the sadistic Romanian Count Dracula, she carried a bit of the Master's modified DNA tucked into her own. On this subject, Renfield believed fully in the gift/curse duality: gifted with an insight into death and the events surrounding it, while cursed to carry the blood marker through which the late Count continues to haunt the family name. Either way, she's come to both appreciate and abhor that truth about herself.

Sensing his levity might damage the camaraderie he'd worked so hard to build with Renfield, Dr. Hedges changed the subject. "Officer over there," Dr. Hedges hooked a thumb over his shoulder, "says he rolled up on the murder in progress, saw the guy go down, the glint of the knife, everything. *Swears* he saw what he saw. But you tell me how he saw this guy alive less than two hours ago."

Renfield snapped on a pair of green latex gloves offered her by Dr. Hedges and crouched beside the body, carefully keeping clear of the brownish puddle of fluids spreading out from beneath the remains.

"The victim's clothes are as degraded as his flesh," Renfield observed. She used her gloved fingers to move aside a layer of heavy cloth that the victim wore. "Look at the intricate needle work here along the edge of this seam."

"I know this symbol; I was once an altar boy," Dr. Hedges exclaimed, fingering the gold thread. "Holy shit! This is the insignia of St. Ignatius! But what the hell happened to him? Is this some precursor to a zombie outbreak or something?"

"Don't go there just yet, Hedgehog." The implications were already making Renfield break out in a cold anxious sweat. She needed to talk to the person in the back of the police cruiser; hopefully they could shed some light on the situation.

"So what happened?" Dr. Hedges asked, but Renfield was already moving out of the alley, stripping her gloves off as she went. She flashed her lanyard at the officer standing guard over the cruiser and opened the back door so she could speak to the woman in the back seat.

"It's about time." Dark and mysterious as her name implied, RedCrow lounged languidly in the back seat of the cruiser, hands zip-tied behind her back.

"Tell me this is not what I think it is, RedCrow."

"Depends on what you think—"

"—It's a wraith," Renfield didn't have the patience for word play, nor was there time. "That is—was—the animated corpse of a priest."

RedCrow nodded solemnly. "Father Ed from St. Ignatius. Word came into the Diablo a couple of days ago of a wraith sighting. Wraiths pray on the faithful, feed on spirit. I went where I knew I'd find both. But Father E…er, I mean the wraith, found me first."

"If you knew about a wraith sighting, you should have contacted Majic immediately. We're a federal entity, resurrected from the past to handle precisely these sorts of things. You are *not* the first line of defense between the worlds, RedCrow."

RedCrow ruffled. "That is exactly what I am, Renfield! I have an inside scoop on what goes on in the dark places of the world. The human race has no idea what reality truly is; most of them couldn't wrap their minds around it if it smacked them in the head."

Renfield knew RedCrow spoke the truth; things did go bump in the night, things that society at large wasn't yet ready to know about. RedCrow was an anomaly herself, the seventh daughter of a seventh daughter, end of her line and last of her kind.

Renfield could only nod in agreement. "I know which side of the fence you're on, RedCrow, so don't take this personally. I've got to let these guys take you in and book you. Trust me," Renfield continued with her hand up to deflect RedCrow's quarrel. "No prosecutor, judge, or jury is going to buy that you killed anyone, not by the condition of those remains. You'll be home by morning."

RedCrow sighed heavily and resigned herself to this. Renfield stepped away from the backseat as the arresting officer stepped in to Mirandize his charge. The medical examiner's van was just closing its back doors on the remains; Dr. Hedges would accompany the body to the morgue until Majic took custody of it.

Dusk was just a memory by the time Renfield approached St. Ignatius alone from a side street. The darkened windows of the historic stone structure looked down on the street like a crotchety old man.

The door at the top of the stairs opened on silent hinges. Renfield slipped inside with respectful silence, hoping her presence would go unnoticed. It took several seconds for her eyes to adjust to the dim light. The air was stale and carried the earthy smell of dry rot, probably due to the ancient crossbeams and worn wooden floorboards. Up near the front of the nave, Renfield could make out heads bent in prayer, but she wasn't sure of their numbers.

A shiver ran the length of Renfield's spine that had nothing to do with the coolness inside the cavernous church. She took a deep breath and brazenly walked past the font without dipping her fingers; those days were long over for her. She slid into a pew not far from the doors. With her hands resting in her lap, the hilt of her own silver blade digging into the small of her back, she bowed her head and peered out from beneath the dark curls that fell into her eyes. She made note of the side entrances, the nooks, and the transept, all the dark places to hide the dead. In a side alcove, the flames of a hundred votives danced at the sculpted feet of Christ.

A square altar of white marble sat at the front of the nave. During the day, the stone alter would be bathed in natural light from the sky light directly above—to resemble the Light of God—but at night, it was an empty black hole, a void through which no Light could shine. Oppressing silence echoed off the walls. The air was close and heavy despite the high, stone walls, perhaps from the guilt that had passed under the transom over the years.

The Master was close; she could feel him pulling at her, tugging at her from inside, their shared DNA humming together, synchronized. The Renfield line, with all its secrets, was as big a part of her makeup as it was a part of her great-great-grandfather's, but she would not let it define her. She refused to answer the Master's dark call, vowed to fight it until she drew her last breath.

Renfield's breath caught in her throat when the confessional door to her left swung open seemingly of its own volition. Was it curiosity, or beckoning from within that drew her from her seat? Renfield slid from the pew. None of the heads bent in prayer seemed to take note of her movement. She crossed the aisle to the confessional where she listened intently for signs that either side of the booth was occupied; there were none. Renfield toed the doors open and found them both empty. Acting on impulse, she stepped inside the visitor's side and pulled the door closed behind her.

The quarters were close and dusty. The velvet fabric covering the walls was threadbare and faded, not from neglect but from use. A stool meant for kneeling was worn from years of prayer. The only sound was Renfield's own blood, rushing in her ears.

The divider between the sides unexpectedly snapped open, causing Renfield to flinch, her heart skipping forward double time. She was sure she'd not heard anyone enter the opposite side of the confessional. Movement there kept her rooted to the spot as she willed herself invisible, not certain which was more the threat: coming face-to-face with a wraith, or with a priest. She suddenly felt like an imposter, trespassing as a former believer.

"In the name of the Father, and of the Son, and of the Holy Spirit," came a paper-dry voice through the screen, followed by an abrasive shock of laughter that shook the confessional. The humorless mirth echoed off the church's stone walls. Renfield's skin reacted with a flush of fire as she felt the full force of the Master's influence roiling in her blood. She would not yield to his will. The pendant grew warm at her throat.

Grizzled gray fingers scrabbled at the screen that separated the sides of the confessional. Renfield pushed to the back of the booth as several hunks of necrotic flesh sloughed off the knuckles, dropping wetly onto the floor. She stifled her gag reflex and a disgusted yelp. The rivets holding the screen in place began to pop free one by one until it crashed to the floor and the arm reached inside, inches from Renfield's face.

Her panic rose to a new level when she tried the handle on her side of the confessional door and found it stuck hard, immovable. The wraith's grasping hand brushed the front of Renfield's shirt, grazing the amulet. A shriek ensued and the arm pulled back.

The amulet—of course! Her father spent his last breath making sure she received it; it had to mean something more than good-bye. Taking a leap of faith, Renfield lifted the talisman from around her neck and shoved it forward through the screen like a probe into the darkness. The wraith shrank away from the amulet's necromancer power, feeling it's eminent demise. Renfield was certain the creature's desperate howl could be heard across the city.

Relying purely on instinct and reaction, Renfield aimed a kick at the stuck door. The impact of her shoe splintered the wood, throwing the door open into the twisted, dead faces of the congregation. She grabbed a votive from a nearby sconce and waved it in front of her. The throng of undead parted before her, shrinking away from the dreaded light. She tossed the votive into the mass as she pushed through the door into the night. Without turning back she ran, feeling the Master's power subsiding.

Renfield didn't stop running until she reached her BMW back at the crime scene. She started the engine and sat behind the wheel, doors locked, until her heart stopped beat-boxing inside her chest. A wraith infestation indeed! Shit just got real. She picked up her cell and reported in to Majic. They would do what they did best and clean up the mess—right under the public's nose—without being seen. Loose ends would be tidied and life would go on. As for Renfield, sleep would continue to be elusive. Because the monsters were real.

## Another Rainy Commute
Larry Anderson

End of a workday, I head home
on exhaust laden 6:30PM city bus.

Driving rain pummels waiting
passengers at street corners
gushes of water from trucks

then the Ross Island Bridge
resisting elements
bearing the weight of each
passenger's day.

I sit in the front seat, a cordial
conversation with a stranger

the startled driver yells "no!",
hits the brakes hard, steers through
a skid, bus hits bridge sidewalk
comes to a stop—I hear him say someone jumped.

The driver jerks the door open
I follow him

we run along the sidewalk
knowing the victim has taken flight—
on one way wings.

I scan intently
over the edge.
I hope somewhere there
is light for him.

We return to the bus,
shaken passengers look

to the driver—he volunteers
nothing.

I watch passengers
as the bus starts moving—

a few resume reading
others look straight ahead
some rest their heads against windows
all silent, reconnecting with their interrupted
after-work torpor.

I'm at the back of the bus,
slowly drifting into indifference—

the bridge far behind
we move in long lines
of shimmering lights, windshield wipers
fending off blowing rain
tires biting wet asphalt.

## Tiny Mr. Spider
Lizzy Welle OeDell

Stumbling upon an unfamiliar smell,
One of abounding aroma, rich as
A decadent mousse, as attractive
As a shiny silver dollar

My eight legs stretched upon recently
Cut grass, sharp blades like
Samurai swords, with each step
My pace became faster

The Misses, she sat on her tuffet,
Creamy whey cuddling her lips,
My mouth became a roaring river,
Dumbfounded, I crept even closer

With fright and fury
Her eyes caught mine,
Seizing the whey she shrieked with speed
And I was left abandoned

## The Year Chickens Wore Underpants

retold by Carrol Haushalter
as recollected by Don Howes of Clark Fork, Idaho

I THINK THE YEAR WAS 1936. We were living in western Iowa near South Dakota. It was the coldest of winters, with temperatures that dropped to thirty degrees below zero for a month at a time, and winds that came howling out of the northwest at about forty-five miles an hour.

During one storm, snow drifted and covered the chicken coop. The coop was twelve feet high and there was at least four or five feet of snow over it. We had to dig a shaft down to the door in order to get inside.

Now, with all that snow on top, the chickens kept quite warm, and for about three weeks they were very happy. They thought it was springtime. They lost their feathers and quit laying eggs. Kernels of corn sprouted up and grew in the cracks between the boards.

In about the third week after the storm, I went to feed the chickens. They were all huddled together on the floor of the coop. They couldn't use the roosts because their feet were so cold that they could not hang on. I ran and told my parents that the chickens were freezing to death.

"How can that be when it's been so blame hot in that chicken house?" Dad asked. They finally figured out that all that heat inside the coop had melted a layer of snow, making a big block of ice around the chicken house. The chickens were now in a deep freeze. Because they had lost all their feathers, they were all standing around turning purple. My parents sent me out on horseback around the neighborhood to gather up all the cold weather clothing I could find. I came back with mostly socks and long johns, and Mother made underpants for all the chickens out of what I had collected. The socks already had holes in the toes, so she simply enlarged them so the chicken's head would go through. Then she cut two holes for the wings and two holes for the legs. She left the backend open, of course, for sanitary reasons.

We finally got the chickens back to a warm state, and it wasn't long before they started laying eggs again. We had about 120 chickens running around wearing socks and long johns of all different colors. We had the most colorful batch of chickens—red, white and green. I wish we had taken a picture of our flock of underwear.

Glen Bledsoe | 19

# FOREVER & ETERNITY

**PART I: THE POLES ARE MELTING. DROUGHTS AND STORMS LASH OUR LANDS. DOES THIS MEAN THE END OF LIFE ON EARTH?**

"I'M AFRAID, TOM."

"WHAT TROUBLES YOU, ANN?"

"I FEAR THE WORLD AS WE KNOW IT..."

"IS ABOUT TO END..."

"FOREVER AND ETERNITY."

20 | Glen Bledsoe

Glen Bledsoe | 21

SHE'S NOTHING BUT A FAKE.
I KNEW YOU WOULD ATTACK HER. SHE IS A VERY SHY PERSON AND DOES NOT WISH TO GAIN WEALTH OR PUBLICITY FOR HER ABILITIES, WHICH SHE CONSIDERS A GIFT FROM A HIGHER POWER.
AS A DEMONSTRATION OF HER TALENTS SHE ASKED ME TO PICK A CARD, WHICH I DID. I RETURNED THE CARD TO THE DECK AND SHE WAS ABLE TO IDENTIFY IT LATER ON ONLY THE SECOND TRY. THAT DEFIES RATIONAL EXPLANATION AS FAR AS I'M CONCERNED, DOCTOR, AND IT IS A FEAT I DARE SCIENCE TO MATCH.
HELLO, POP!
HELLO, ANN. HOW NICE TO SEE YOU.
HAVE YOU SAVED THE WORLD YET, POP?

NOW WHAT MAKES YOU THINK THIS OLD WORLD NEEDS SAVING?
OH, I HEAR THINGS. I KNOW THE WORLD IS OVERHEATING.
NONSENSE. THE WORLD WILL GO ON TURNING TOMORROW, AND THE DAY AFTER THAT AND THE DAY AFTER THAT. THERE'S NOTHING TO WORRY YOUR LITTLE HEAD OVER. D'YOU HEAR ME?
YES, POPPA.
WEEKS PASS. CLIMATE DISASTER CONTINUES WITHOUT PAUSE CAUSING UNCALCULATED GRIEF AND MISFORTUNATE FOR THE PEOPLE OF PLANET EARTH. AT LAST, MADAME ZORNE ARRIVES AT WRIGHT LABS.
I AM THINKING THERE IS A NONBELIEVER AMONG US.
NOT ME. I BELIEVE.
NOT ME EITHER.
IT'S NOT ME. I BELIEVE. I MENTIONED MADAME IN MY PRAYERS JUST LAST NIGHT. ASK ANN IF YOU DON'T BELIEVE ME.
GOOD. IF YOU DON'T BELIEVE THEN YOU'RE JUST A SAPPY HEADED SCIENTIST WHO ALWAYS WANTS PROOF. SO TONIGHT WE WILL ATTEMPT TO CONTACT THE OTHER SIDE FOR THE ADVICE YOU SEEK. I WILL TRY NOT TO GET ECTOPLASM ON THE LADIES' DRESSES, BUT BE ADVISED THIS COULD GET MESSY.

THIS IS GOING TO BE GREAT FUN, EH ANN?
OH, YES.
WHOA! I'M SO PICKING UP SOMETHING.
ECTOPLASM! GROSS!
THAT'S JUST WRONG.
EEEWWW! DISGUSTING!
IT LOOKS MORE LIKE A HANKY TO ME.
THAT'S MICHAEL JACKSON IN THE ECTOPLASM.
QUIET, EVERYONE! MICHAEL HAS SOMETHING TO SAY TO US.
HI, FRIENDS. THIS IS MICHAEL SPEAKING TO YOU FROM CELESTIAL NEVERLAND.
EARTH IS IN BIG TROUBLE. YOU NEED HELP.
I WILL SPEAK TO MY ALIEN FRIENDS AND SEE WHAT CAN BE DONE.

PART II: AND SO THE APPEAL IS SENT ACROSS THE AETHER TO A WORLD OF ENLIGHTENED BEINGS THAT MICHAEL MET ON A TOUR OF THE UNIVERSE. WHILE POSSESSING GREAT POWER, THESE CREATURES HAVE DEVELOPED A RATHER CAVALIER ATTITUDE TOWARDS SPECIES WHO ARE UNABLE TO ACT IN THEIR OWN BEST INTERESTS. HONESTLY, CAN YOU BLAME THEM?
BEHOLD THE PLANET B-MUSE.
MICHAEL SENDS US A PLEA TO ASSIST THE PEOPLE OF HIS WORLD.
WHAT IS THE NAME OF THIS WORLD?
EARTH.
NEVER HEARD OF IT.
IT IS THE PLANET THAT INVENTED TWINKIES.
WHY HAVE WE NOT DESTROYED THEM ALREADY?
NO NEED. THEY ARE DESTROYING THEMSELVES.
CAN WE WATCH?
BAD ATTITUDE THERE, ARKGOST.

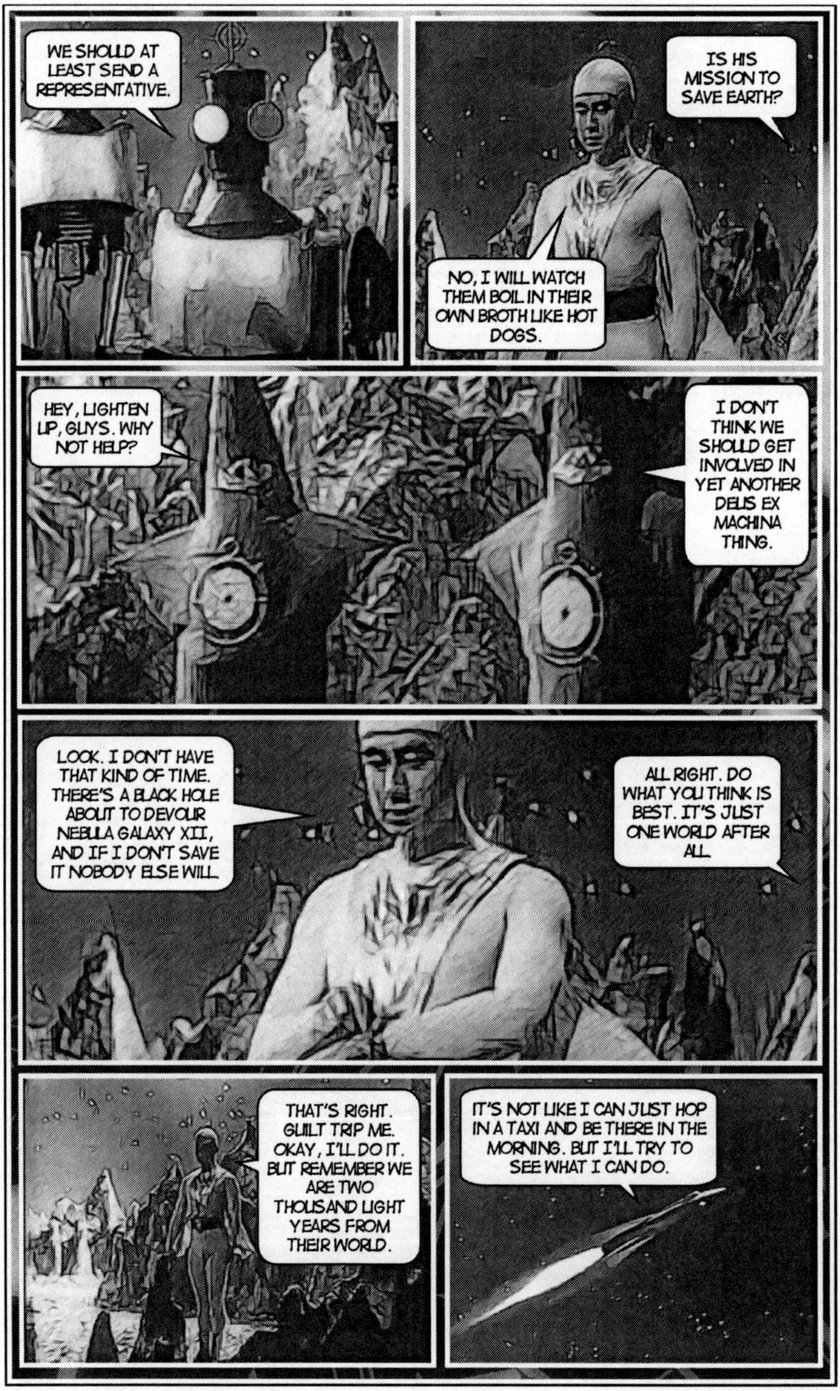
WE SHOULD AT LEAST SEND A REPRESENTATIVE.
IS HIS MISSION TO SAVE EARTH?
NO, I WILL WATCH THEM BOIL IN THEIR OWN BROTH LIKE HOT DOGS.
HEY, LIGHTEN UP, GUYS. WHY NOT HELP?
I DON'T THINK WE SHOULD GET INVOLVED IN YET ANOTHER DEUS EX MACHINA THING.
LOOK. I DON'T HAVE THAT KIND OF TIME. THERE'S A BLACK HOLE ABOUT TO DEVOUR NEBULA GALAXY XII, AND IF I DON'T SAVE IT NOBODY ELSE WILL.
ALL RIGHT. DO WHAT YOU THINK IS BEST. IT'S JUST ONE WORLD AFTER ALL.
THAT'S RIGHT. GUILT TRIP ME. OKAY, I'LL DO IT. BUT REMEMBER WE ARE TWO THOUSAND LIGHT YEARS FROM THEIR WORLD.
IT'S NOT LIKE I CAN JUST HOP IN A TAXI AND BE THERE IN THE MORNING. BUT I'LL TRY TO SEE WHAT I CAN DO.

Glen Bledsoe | 27

YEAH, I COULD PROBABLY MAKE TIME IF YOU REALLY WANT ME TO.
YOU GIRLS KNOW A LITTLE PLACE WHERE WE CAN CATCH A BITE TO EAT?
HOW CAN YOU THINK OF FOOD AT A TIME LIKE THIS?
POINT TAKEN. WE CAN ALWAYS GRAB SOMETHING LATER.
LET US BEGIN WITH A CEREMONIAL MASSAGE.
HOLD ON. LET ME SPLASH ON A LITTLE COLOGNE. I'LL BE RIGHT WITH YOU.
FIN

# The Castle

John Sibley Williams

THE WORLD WAS BLUE FOR a moment, foreign, inescapable. All the men I might become vanished within the wave's eclipse, which stole the sun and all its promise, stole the sand and my family and the other children's rollicking voices. Gelatinous arms from a hidden deep snared my legs and pulled me down, further, begged me join their unchanging universe, without history or future, just blind steady drifting upon currents that moved together in one direction, away. The ghosts I'd gathered over my nine short years were there, below me, around me, wrapped greenly around my thighs. I thought I might stay. They seemed happy enough, which was more than I could claim of my dry life sandwiched between parents who battled their misplaced love with the barbs and blades of silence.

But the wave kicked back, returned me to the faded gray summer and overcrowded boardwalk of childhood. Arms released their grasp. The ghosts hushed in that way ghosts have, leaving you to question if they'd ever really existed, held you tight and then abandoned you. Coating my skin, meaty slabs of kelp and biting salt. I washed what I could from my body, which had been given back to me. The popcorn vendors continued to toss sealed bags of their wares to dollar-waving children. Balloons continued to pop from the force of darts and luck. And the sandpipers—always grouped, never alone—cut aluminum streaks from the sky.

Around me, constant movement and what seemed, for the first time, like a hollowness. I'm made for something different, I thought. I'll be happier. I looked to my parents, who had fallen asleep beneath gigantic canopies that blocked the light. Their hands dangled loosely at their sides without touching. Happier, yes, and I'll know love.

That was the moment we met. Not a few seconds after I'd planned the entirety of my life. A voice rustled from behind me. Are you alright?, it asked, barely discernible from the sea breeze. The words paused there, repeating themselves. Are you...alright?

I turned my back to the water and met the sun head on. Somewhere within it, the outline of a face blackened by proximity, featureless, marooned on the surface of light. At that moment, it could have been anyone—parent, lifeguard, ghost, angel, in all of which I still believed. I crunched my eyes into tiny brown half-moons and leveled my hand over them, to focus. There were lips, at first, wire-thin lips, almost the absence of lips, that curled up into an ivory line of teeth, with a gap in front that whistled out consonants, birdlike and resonant. And a chin, ever so slightly dimpled, and skin the chalky color of some silent film actress.

"I saw you out there, alone, and thought you weren't coming back."

And a nose, diminutive, not imposing itself, perfectly buttoned between cheeks rubbed raw by the wind and left slightly aglow. I'd seen sand like that in Arizona, where I grew up, where we moved from a few years before. Sand that held the light long after evening. Sand that if you dug up layer upon layer with your desperately curious child-hands, even with a spade, even with a bulldozer, still you'd find color. So far down, to the center. I never dug all the way to China, but I'd seen pictures in dusty library copies of National Geographic that showed similar sands in Mongolia. I simply knew the light never stopped. It saturated every level and couldn't be un-dug. I wanted to play naked in her cheeks, with nothing around but the background dance of rattlers and color, and keep moving deeper into her, to see if I was right about eternity.

"You scared me."

And the pale luminescence of her eyes. Hints of charcoal smoke and clouds after the rains had passed.

"You scared me. I thought you were gone."

She must have been about my age, perhaps a year older. Her speck of a body wrapped in a dry one-piece. I pictured her blowing about aimlessly on the wind. Unimaginably weightless. A blank sheet of paper rising and falling with the currents. Folding in upon itself and straightening out. I reached for the paper, to return it to earth.

"But you're here now; you're okay." She leaned into me, sexless body against sexless body, and untwined a bit of seaweed from my hair.

The world paused its comings and goings. The pretzels suspended mid-rotation in their glass cages. Frisbees ceased spinning and, along with the frozen kites, cut strange, foreboding shapes into the motionless sky. She smelled like nothing, absolutely nothing but the environment around us. I wanted to dig. I wanted light. I'd never seen it in a person before.

"What's your name?" she asked, still bent across me, brushing sand from my shoulder. "Can you...speak?"

The world gently began to move, in slow motion, in cloud time. A pelican spent a full minute wafting its wings overhead, a full hour rising into the sky. She reclined from me in what might have been a month and exhausted a lifetime replanting her feet in the sand. The world was blue again, but not foreign. Things I never knew had been stolen were suddenly there, painted on my eyelids, obvious and illuminated: the moment, which I'd never cared much to live in, and the future, its promise. I saw myself as an old man, suspendered and spectacled, painted wooden ducks on the mantle, the fire below it fighting off winter. And I pictured her, at sixty, at two hundred, at fifteen, beneath a huge canopy, hand dangling by her side, clasped in mine.

The universe found its speed again. The Frisbees landed and kites ripped through the clouds. The pelican was gone. My parents still hadn't woken. I realized I was wrong about the hollowness. And I realized I had a voice.

"I love you."


Emily and I consumed the waning summer days as if nobody and nothing else existed, and we met little resistance from the outside world, which hardly troubled with the grandiose plans of youth. Though we lived on opposite ends of town, separated by nearly ten miles of drugstores and soda fountains and neon-lit gas stations, we carefully wove excuses to see each other. Excuses that seemed cloaked in impetuousness and nativity. Nobody guessed our real motivations for suddenly, at that very moment, without taking no for an answer, needing to taste a certain brand of ice cream, only sold in one shop, or needing to visit a certain museum, in my case one dedicated to the completion of the transcontinental railroad, which sat blocks from her home, where she would be waiting.

"You're becoming quite the brat," one of my parents would say, followed by a chuckle from the other, followed by one, sometimes both, taking me where I demanded. Easier than instigating an argument. Their collapses seemed clear enough.

Sometimes their work schedules wouldn't allow it, and I'd un-retire my little silver beast, a BMX racer, and cycle the town, to its southern outskirts, to the cottage her mother rented, and lay sweaty and flat in the overgrown tulip bed waiting for her to sense me waiting. I never waited long. I let the clouds overhead shape into whatever they chose, often misshaped hearts. I covered my shirtless body in fallen flower petals and pretended I'd died in her absence, died from her absence. It was one of our many games. She'd drop her mouth into a silent scream, clasp her arms to her chest, hands over heart, and stand like that until I smiled. She never had to wait long.

But mainly our trysts were less suspicious, our secrets best hidden in daylight, beneath a thousand pairs of eyes. We convinced our parents that the beach, the same beach that nearly drowned me, was our holy land. I'd race into their bedroom while dawn still woke and pull the sheets from their fully-clothed, separate bodies, demanding, as if by sudden inspiration, as if my last breaths were imminent, that the sands were calling to me and we had to leave that second. And the sands were calling to me. When I dreamt of Emily, it was always on that beach, haloed in sun.

It was the first weekend of September, the beach packed end-to-end with summer's well wishers, all waving farewell to indulgence and freedom, when we built the castle. The tide was receding, leaving behind cool glassy sand that squirmed between our toes and stuck there, white and hardened, in firm surgical casts.

"We need to build something," I said. "Something to escape into. Somewhere to hide."

"It's all over, isn't it?" Emily replied to no one in particular, face tilted toward the sea, which was too cold to swim, which was running from us. "We're leaving soon, Mom and I. Back to Boise. It's so dry there, so far from things." She returned there in her mind and sighed just like my mother did each morning over breakfast, eyes permanently set in some personal elsewhere. "And who knows what'll happen next year? What if we don't come back?"

The blue eclipsed me again. Those same underwater tentacles. Those same ghosts. That same fear of things never changing, alongside the safety of inertia.

"I'll still be here, Emily. I'm not going anywhere." And I meant it. I may still have been weeks from taking on a second digit, and only children take themselves seriously, but I meant it. Everything was black and white. The scattered half-broken shells absent their crab bodies. The shucked oysters. The planks of the boardwalk that led on and on and on, eventually into nothing. Like everything else: adult conversation, devotion, warmth. Even my dreams, hued in Arizona sands, were in hindsight as chromatic as an old film. And as silent. Things simply had to make sense in such elementary terms. All the way down to China.

"Maybe. But we'll be older. We'll be different people. You'll forget me or I'll forget you. We've never even kissed."

"So let's kiss," I attempted. I'd never connected physicality to love before.

I let the film reel roll through its spools, cast its light on the screen. We were bigger than life, by ourselves, beneath so many disinterested eyes.

"It's not the right time."

She said all this to the sea. She was every age but nine. She was four hundred and twelve. She was thirty-two. I touched her hand. I wanted to make each other timeless, to live in a single moment forever.

Clouds banded together in armies above us. The crowds began to collect their unused towels and hibernate for the season. It would not get warm again for many months. The sand was like snow before the ice arrives, perfect for dreaming and building.

We both stared into each other, then around us, at nothing, then deeper into each other again. Someone was calling me from down the beach, from another world. I recognized the voice as if from my past. And everyone I'd ever met before that moment was of the past.

I sank to my knees, sank my hands into the wet grains, cupped them together into an imperfect rectangle a few inches high, edges smoothed over. Flattening the top, I looked up at Emily and said, "This is our bed."

Silence.

"Don't you see it? We're sleeping right here, next to each other. Don't you see it?"

She spun her eyes from the retreating water and stared for a long time at our bed. Beige-sheeted. Comfortable as cloud and earth. I tucked the blanket up to my chin and waited for her to join me. I drifted in and out of sleep, waiting. The other side of the bed grew cold. My fingers absentmindedly traced the curves of where her indent should be. I looked up at the plaster ceiling, a few polished cedar beams exposed. I placed a fan in the center and let the air move around me. The radiator hissed and smelled like something old rediscovering its use. I wondered what curtains she'd choose. I guessed pale blue, the blue of sky and sea, the blue hidden within white, exposed when light strikes it just right.

"I see it," she chirped, wind-like but confident.

"Do you?"

"I do. I see it." The beach emptied, completely, of even our parents and the sun. "Should we have a staircase? One of those long staircases that look like a two-headed snake? That just keep going up and up? That start as two but become one in the end?"

The bed warmed. We threw the blanket over our heads and poked each other and laughed and shone flashlights in our open mouths until autumn peeked out through our cheeks, decked in tangerine phosphorescence and mystery.

"Sure we can. All the staircases in the world. They're all right there." I pointed down the hall, into the emptiness, and suddenly there were staircases.

Our pink hands, slick with sand and movement, worked hard, gathered timber and nails, chandeliers, plates, bricks for the fireplace, pillows for the bed, crown molding, tea sets and then different tea sets, curtains as blue as I'd hoped, photos for the mantle, everything we'd ever seen in a house, things we hadn't words for but knew by smell, taste, tactile things like hardwood floors, wallpaper. Everything from tiny fistfuls of sand that assumed significance as soon as we named them. "Doorbell." And suddenly the grand foyer echoed with song. "Umbrella." And suddenly a pair of them, and a silver stand to hold them, and rain outside, seen through the lace-rimmed windows that looked out simultaneously upon both sea and mountain, desert and pine forest, with snakes and deer and polar bears wandering the lawn, and kids who shared our adult faces, though more hers than mine.

Once we'd perfected the house, planted the carpets, let the paint dry, I swept my hand in some grandiose gesture of showmanship and said, "Ladies first!" And we entered the castle. Upon locking the door behind us, childhood vanished. And the pelican. The sea spray. The distant voices calling us back joined the ghosts, with their temporary arms and forgotten lessons, their need to embrace and never let go, to change us by teaching how they've never changed. We were alone in our house, far from the beach. In time we'd forget the foundation was made of sand.

Exhausted, terrified but certain, sweaty, content, we pounced into bed and curled ourselves into a pair of quotation marks, inches apart. One of us sighed. The other was already dreaming away, far away from the room. Perhaps back to that sea of youth, that could never be revisited. The fan swooshed overhead. Chilled, we chose our sides of the bed and the positions we'd never budge from. I remember us both smiling, half-elsewhere, in a castle we'd fashioned from hope. Inches apart. Quotation marks. Waiting for the word that would come between us.

And we slept like that, without waking, for thirty-five years.

A cut of light. Translucent daybreak. An open window breeze. A gold-rimmed horizon.

The brute force of morning warmed our eyes open, simultaneously. I swallowed all the oxygen in the room in a single yawn. It was as if we hadn't moved, as if not a few moments has passed since we'd met, so long ago, on a beach we had different memories of. The bed had tired of our constant warmth and cooled to an autumn tingle playing itself up our spines. We both shivered and looked at each other. Not into. At. As if for the last first time.

The story of what happened those shared decades of sleep was written in her eyes. Her irises had faded like over-washed plates. Less the gray of clouds now, after the rains. More the gray of cityscape and routine, awaiting yet another storm.

She rolled into the foreign body beside her. "Watch out, don't forget I'm still here," I replied to her shoulder, which burrowed into my adult chest, downy-haired and thick. "I haven't forgotten," was all she said.

"I don't really remember anything from before," I countered. "Our life's been a blanket of years. Soft enough, comfortable, but spread thin. You know? How did we get here?"

The taste of salt returned, as if from someone else's memory. I picked out the smell of oysters from the thousand scents coursing through the window. Then my father's aftershave on my neck. She still retained the odor of absence.

"You don't remember our wedding? Our son's birth? Your mother's death? It's like you to have dreamed yourself away from things, that's partly why I fell in love with you, but not everything that matters!" The fire in her eyes returned, that fire I loved in its infancy, when it flamed blue into the falling summer sun.

"We were on a beach, right? You saved me from something."

Individual pieces that didn't interlock, without their puzzle. Perhaps I'd never made it out of the sea's mouth that morning when I was a child. Perhaps I continued to live in the arms of ghosts, my parents' arms.

"Yeah, I saved you from yourself. Who knows where you'd have ended up, what flights of fancy would have lifted those silly wings of yours, if I hadn't grounded you again. You used to call me your savior, remember? Your angel."

"I still do, every day," I murmured.

"Exactly. You do. Every day. At the end of every conversation. Just like your father used to. Remember how the words raked down your mother's back? How they had grown to mean something else entirely?"

But I was already elsewhere. I was walking backwards through myself to find where our plans had curved off their path. "Do you remember building the house? It was on the seashore, no? Our hands grew dirty with it all, with constructing life from a dream."

"I haven't looked outside in so long," Emily said to the window, half in response. Her skin had ashened over the years. The sunlight cut through it like paper until she blended with the bed. And her voice, that voice once inseparable from the calm sea, had become that of growling waves against hard rock.

"Everything was perfect, wasn't it?" I asked the back of her head.

Silence. And a bit of light goldening her hair.

"Where are you right now, my angel? Back on the beach?"

She turned to me with that blank amnesiac look of the dreamer plucked too early from her dream. Our hands dangled loosely beside each other and almost touched. The angle of our gigantic roof blocked the sun. Our boy was off somewhere nearly drowning in his own current, being saved, and forgetting again how to swim.

Then Emily said, as if in prayer, "I...don't think we ever left."

The boardwalk looked like it had been closed for a lifetime when we left the castle we'd built from sand and wandered together, for the first time since childhood, down its beach. The sand door slammed behind us, though the wind was delicate and undemanding. The pelican had flown, if it ever existed, and our families were as absent as the shops. Nothing spun from grilling racks and sweated into a river of grease. No bags of popcorn were thrown to us. All the umbrellas had tumbled over like so many colorful whales paused mid-breech, the surface below them permanently ruptured.

"There are no words for it, are there?" one of us asked.

"And no answers," the other replied.

I reached out to touch her hand but ended up holding my own. She clasped her body tight and shivered with the sky.

We walked like that for a few more years, down the beach where we met, the castle distancing itself with each step. The wind gathered its strength.

We turned back to measure the miles between where we once lived and the foreignness of where we found ourselves. The waves had erased the castle and our footsteps leading away from it. When I pointed at a mound of primrose and said "threshold", nothing changed. It remained primrose.

One of us knelt down and began gathering sand into pillars, flattening it into beds, carving from fingernails paper-thin staircases that wound together at the top. The other one, if I remember correctly, waded through the empty blue sea, with its green arms and voices, then further out into its familiar, unchanging universe.

## Untitled Poem
K. D. Schmidt

The sun casts amber glow across the horizon
As the season transitions
We experience
The scent of earth in retirement
The sight of children waiting for school buses
The taste of ripe fruit tugged from the tree
The smoke from fields cleansed by fire
As we prepare
For winter

# Grieving Mallards

Pattie PalmerBaker

The female mallard takes a fighter's stance
weaves and bobs
her quacks smack the air with body punches.
*I'm the one you want,*
*me, I'm the one.*
She lifts off arcing away
from the grass-shrouded hillside
the swoosh of her wings hiss her meaning
*nothing*
*not a thing lies hidden*
*in the ferns dotting the uphill.*

Two feathered rockets
one dappled dun one teal glinted black
shoot toward the river, yank prying eyes
away from the eggs cached in knee high grass.
Both quack until their fear breaks the air.
*Don't look don't look*
where the eggs gleam alabaster.

Through green lattice the raccoon spies oval aglow.
With delicate fingers she pries open the shell
sucks and licks the orange globe the clear pool.
The coyote doesn't need to look
he sniffs the air the ground
his jaws unhinge his mouth plucks the egg
one crunch the egg shatters
one gulp he swallows.

They trudge up the hill
the female's eyes shuttered
her beak brushing the curve of the male's black tail feathers
her feet slap flat
mirror his steps as he traces slow S curves.

*All is lost, all is lost*
the eggshells and the slime of life
only a slick shines in the hollowed-out nest.

# Through Sun Or Storm
Devon Seale

It had been a long time. Too long perhaps, since Jaithron had ventured forth from the dusty confines of his library. Too long since he had taken the first steps on a new journey. Despite the dark times, and the reasons he had chosen to finally set out, he was, in a way, glad. Glad to be out in the fresh air. Glad to experience the world once more beyond the experiences he often gathered through the tales others brought to him.

Not that there was anything to be glad about. The kingdom was at war. Several kingdoms were at war. Normally, he would be trying to gather memories and records of these events, as he had always done. From the confines of his library he had reached out with his thoughts and watched much of the war develop. However, the situation required more than that now. He would have more to write down later, more memories to keep safe by the time his trek was done. But that was not the focus of this journey. His success meant life or death for possibly thousands of individuals.

It was rare—even for him—to have the chance to so thoroughly examine the memories of one of the enemy, and he had to get what he'd learned to those who could use it. He had to do so quickly, and he had to do so secretly. Sending this information telepathically over such a long distance—carried, perhaps, through the minds of several other dragons in order to extend the range of the broadcast—could end up with it being intercepted by one of the enemy's strong telepaths. No, this information needed to be carried in person to its destination. It was far too vital, and the element of surprise his kingdom would have because of it could prove invaluable.

The bright sun warmed Jaithron's purple scales. For just a moment he paused, allowing himself to enjoy the sensation. It was not something he felt very often these days. His duties in the library, and his telepathic strategy for handling his duties as Memory Keeper, saw to it that he remained indoors most of the time. Sad, when he thought about it. Dragons weren't supposed to be inside so much. Perhaps he had best rethink the way he handled his duties.

Taking a deep breath, he stretched his wings, gave a couple slow flaps, and then launched himself into the air. He climbed for a few minutes, circled the castle, then banked toward the east, accelerating as quickly as possible. Thanks to a good tailwind, he suspected that his trip wouldn't take more than a few hours. Assuming the weather didn't change, of course.

An hour after he left the castle, Jaithron found himself in the middle of a raging storm. Rain beat down on him, soaking his scales and making it hard to see. High-speed winds threatened to throw him off course. He fought against these challenges, twisting and turning through the turbulence, then finally angled himself upward. Perhaps he could get above the clouds and find clear skies again. Why hadn't he thought of that sooner?

An unexpected blast of wind hit him hard, sending him spinning through the air before he could breach the cloud layer. Out of control and unable to compensate, he folded his wings and let himself fall, angling his nose toward the ground. Closing his eyes, he felt out the wind direction; tried to calculate its changes; waited for the right moment.

With a twist, he turned to face the incoming wind and snapped his wings open, arching back up into actual flight. He flapped hard against the onslaught, slowly gaining headway. He had lost a lot of altitude, but at least he was still in the air. The storm was so powerful, however, that he finally decided it was unsafe to fly. So much for a fast trip to deliver his information, but safety came first. He couldn't deliver anything if he was dead.

Buffeting downward as he tried to change direction with the wind, he scanned the ground below, looking for shelter. His eyes finally came to rest on what looked to be the entrance of a small cave. He tucked his wings in once again and dove, heading toward it. The wind pushed against him from every direction, and just as he was about to reach his destination, another rogue gust caught him and sent him spinning off, away from the opening. Turning toward the cave and releasing his wings, he regained control and finally landed at the opening to his chosen shelter. He quickly crawled in to wait out the storm.

Jaithron was forced to linger in the cave for over an hour, counting the minutes and hoping that this delay would not prove detrimental to his mission. If he was too late…If this sudden storm meant the loss of the war…Such a fate was unacceptable. He would simply have to move faster.

When the storm had finally calmed, Jaithron emerged from the cave and saw that clouds still covered the sky, though not as densely as before. The rain was now a peaceful drizzle, and the wind had slowed to a gentle breeze. Now he could travel again, and travel he did.

Taking flight, he climbed quickly into the air, his wings working harder than they had in years as he weaved his way through the light rainclouds, trying to make up for the time he had lost to the storm. Silently he cursed whatever luck had brought the storm his way and wondered at its sudden appearance. He had concerns that some other dragon could have created it to delay him…though there was no way anyone could know what he was up to. He had told no one before departing, and the prisoner he had scanned was trapped in a dungeon cell, unable to send a word of warning. In all reality, it was likely a natural occurrence. The weather in that area was certainly capable of changing without warning.

Pushing these thoughts aside, he focused on his flight. He had to be nearing the army now. Scanning the ground, he watched for signs of the military force he sought. He could clearly see the path they had taken, the marks of their travel etched into the land below. No matter how hard they tried not to, large armies always left a trail. It was inevitable with so many traveling at once. Only flight could allow such a force to move without marking the land, and only some of their army could fly, for not all were dragons.

He spotted them at last. It was a large force, boasting hundreds of solders of various species. Dragons were mixed in with centaurs, humans, satyrs, and minotaurs, with other species mixed in as well. Relief flooded through Jaithron when he saw that the army seemed to be intact. The area was calm at the moment. No enemy in sight. The army was moving at an even pace, but it was easy enough for him to overtake them. Beginning his descent, he scanned the troops for signs of his king. His news would go directly to King Erickson. No one else could be trusted; not with this information.

Small, white, and devoid of scales due to his hybrid blood, King Erickson marched at the front of the army. He had always been a hands-on leader, ordering nothing that he himself wouldn't be willing to do if necessary. It was a rare trait in a king, but perhaps it was what made him so successful. Jaithron landed a short distance ahead of King Erickson and rested a moment while the king signaled his army to halt and then approached. Jaithron got straight to the point.

"Your Majesty, we need to talk. There is a spy in your army."

The smile that had been spreading across King Erickson's muzzle immediately disappeared. "That's a pretty serious bit of intelligence, Jaithron. Care to tell me who?"

"I'm afraid I don't know, your Majesty. Only that there is one, and this means your force could very well be walking straight into a trap at any time." Jaithron's mind started going over the possibilities, while King Erickson glanced back at the lines of soldiers, probably thinking the same thing. Who could it be? Jaithron had another question for himself, though. Why hadn't he thought it over on the way? He had had plenty of time thanks to that sudden storm.

His first thought was the black dragon, Kaidar, who had once worked for the enemy, but the circumstances of his changing sides made him a highly unlikely suspect. Others among the leaders had been working for years to keep their kingdom safe, making them equally unlikely. Most of the regular soldiers had grown up in their kingdom. That, and their lower ranks, made them less likely to be working for the enemy. A spy would need a position of authority if he were to gather the information he'd need for his masters.

King Erickson headed back toward the army, to discuss the matter with his advisers. Jaithron decided there was only one way to be sure. Telepathically, he began probing the mix of creatures that made up this military, checking each mind for signs of subterfuge. He would find the culprit himself. He started with the king's advisers and slowly worked his way through the ranks, moving quickly but efficiently from mind to mind.

Centuries of practice allowed him to slip through their thoughts undetected, save but a very few. The golden dragon, Arlana, recognized his contact, of course, but realized his purpose and did not resist. He was unsurprised by her awareness. Young as she was, at least compared to himself, she had been trained by him. He might have been disappointed if she hadn't noticed him. The only other individual to show awareness was another dragon, one he wasn't as familiar with who—

Jaithron was suddenly forced to go on the defensive as this new mind attacked, striking hard toward his consciousness. He quickly built up a mental barrier, barring the dragon's access, and then jabbed once more himself. This must be the spy. It was the only explanation. More than that, the dragon was also old. Not as old as Jaithron, but old enough and experienced enough to put up a strong fight. Jaithron was forced to adjust his barrier as the enemy tried to break through a weak point at the edge of his thoughts. The spy was very experienced, indeed.

Jaithron found himself pushing back and forth with this enemy, attacking then retreating, only to attack again from another direction. He was certain now; this was the spy he'd been looking for. This was the enemy's upper hand in the war, and it needed to be stopped. This adversary was taking up enough of Jaithron's concentration that he was unable to divert any of his attention to the outside world. He couldn't warn the others. This was his fight now.

Going on the offensive, Jaithron stabbed out with his thoughts, forcing the enemy to withdraw back behind his solid, mental barriers. Jaithron probed along the borders of the enemy's mind, seeking any weakness, any crack in the defenses. There were none. This dragon had obviously been well trained and had plenty of experience. It was no wonder that this spy had been chosen to infiltrate their army. Certainly Jaithron could eventually break through his defenses, but it would take far too long, and if he wasn't careful, a telepath of this caliber could undermine him while he was focused. Better to outwit the enemy than to overwhelm.

Following this train of thought, Jaithron feigned a weakened series of mental strikes. The dragon took the bait and Jaithron quickly withdrew. Not fast enough. The enemy got into his thoughts. Quickly, Jaithron diverted the assault, guiding it to a less important portion of his memories and blocking off everything else from the enemy's view. This done, he linked his thoughts with the invading mental probe and created a feedback loop, trailing his own probe up the link of the enemy's and right past the other dragon's defenses.

He was in.

Before the other dragon could recognize what had happened, Jaithron seized control, quickly moving through the other mind and undermining all of its defenses, checking and double-checking to ensure that the same trick was not used on him. In his overconfidence, the other dragon had let Jaithron right in. Keeping his adversary paralyzed, Jaithron sifted through his thoughts, gleaning memories and scanning information. Yes, this was the spy, and a trap had most definitely been set. Another two days and King Erickson's entire army would have been surrounded.

His task done, Jaithron needed to do only one other thing. This enemy was too dangerous, his telepathic potential too powerful. He couldn't be left alive. Though he would have preferred otherwise, Jaithron was left to the task of preventing any further trouble. Reaching further into the enemy's mind, he reworked the subconscious sectors that controlled bodily functions, allowing the heart to simply…stop. He could sense the other's struggle to regain control, but refused to relent, instead recording this dragon's thoughts for future reference. There was no point in wasting the memories. As a Memory Keeper, it was his task to keep such things safe, after all.

He waited for a long moment, ensuring the demise of the other dragon. Somewhere out in the field there was a roar of pain as the spy dragon died. Jaithron withdrew back to his own mind before any of his own consciousness was damaged by the other's death. He found himself surrounded by a number of others, including both King Erickson and Arlana. His silent battle had left him frozen for several minutes and the look of concern etched over their faces told him they'd noticed. Their expressions became even more serious at the sound of the enemy's death throes.

Before anyone could ask him anything, Jaithron fed the tactical information he'd gathered from his opponent straight into King Erickson's thoughts, giving him the enemy's entire strategy. It was the king's job to deal with it now. The war would go on, but this army now stood a much better chance of not only surviving, but of outwitting the enemy in a way previously impossible.

After a moment, Jaithron took to the air and headed back towards home. The fields of battle were not the place for a scholar. He would gather their battle stories when they returned. And return they would. He had no doubt of that. No, it was better now to return to the dusty confines of his library, where his new memories could be safely recorded for future generations.

# Lake
Lizzy Welle OeDell

Rippling waters
Fashioned by gusts that
Rush from the mouth
Of the sky like the
Bus on the first day of school.

Sitting in your backyard
The mountain guards you,
Crystals glisten under close watch
And adventurism locked within
Your depths.

What more do your depths hold?
Finicky fish planning a worm revolt,
Seaweed swaying like storm struck
Guests on ship,
Tackle lost from drunken men
Unable to tie their hooks,
Or
The key to ultimate escape,
Tranquil, serene, resembling a dream
Pulling me closer, calling my name,
Like echoes from my desires.
You are the lake that embraces it all.

## Advice For The Artist's Husband
Pattie PalmerBaker

You are not her dream love.
She holds out for an amber-eyed chimera
whose winged-embrace twice enfolds her
flash-fires her body scatters her platinum ash.

Don't tell her not to worry
to meditate up the nirvana stairs
nothing is real.
She names into existence everything you deny
and at night she dreams real people
breaks bail for the best offer.

Don't try to tell her anything
especially how to live her life how to love her life
or how to kill her enemies
because she knows everything.

She may ask you to suggest a color
or an image-arrangement in one of her collages.
She won't follow your advice
best not to take it personally
although you did know best.

And remember
dinner is not always on time
often leftovers lukewarm
but arranged to fill your eye.

## Jamie G. Has Changed

Angie Hughes

Going ten years without visiting with my extended family was a mistake. The shock of seeing my cousin for the first time since the wedding of another family member about sent me into fits of gawky, giddy schoolgirl convulsions. I asked my sister, "Who is that guy with the dreadlocks," to which she replied, "Jamie." Feeling completely out of my element and as if I had entered a strange episode of The Twilight Zone, I said in a voice I don't usually use, "You must be mistaken." She looked at me with a funny, curled up lip and snorted. "That's him. I guess you've missed the last couple of camping reunions."

There he was, half naked, up to his thighs in freezing cold river water, pulling the hair band out of his mass of red curls, dreads, and debris. He was now a small strawberry slice of the boy I once knew and my mind spun and whirred as I felt a distance from him and these people that I had never experienced before. Even in my most uncomfortable moments, when I stood awkwardly in the corner at holiday gatherings, pulling at my too-tight designer sweater, not yet fully able to maneuver a familial social scene, I had never felt so alone in the midst of this clan. This was the kind of distance where one is completely and electively left out of the loop, then returns after a long absence and realizes that something very important was missed—with no chance for retrieval. I would have liked to witness this transformation and I arrived too late, cheated. As Jamie glided through the water, comfortable in the skin of his new confident and sexually aware self, I looked on in awe, glad that my sunglasses were masking my watchful and curious eye.

Over the years, I had heard talk of drugs, skanky girls, meltdowns, and meth-dealing out of a souped-up shiny blue car; what now stood before me was too lovely and fragile and strikingly different to come anywhere close to that messy persona of a drug pusher that I had built up in my mind. Looking at his seemingly vegan nourished body, ribs protruding, I wondered if I had somehow missed something in my own life and the thought crossed my mind that maybe I was half alive and he had it all right. His ease in the water told all those watching from the rocky shore that no matter his profession or past, he was in charge here. Jamie had shed all that chubby red baby fat, the ill-fitted khakis, a perpetual bang-cut across the forehead and was now a thirty-something-year-old MAN. Delicate, and yet electrifyingly grounded and present, his slight frame seemed brimming full of a decade's worth of secrets and experiences. I was jealous, mystified, and enraptured all at the same time. Regardless of the hell that he might have been through, or perhaps put his family through, I could tell that he knew who he was—and he was deliciously free in this river.

# Contributors

**Larry Anderson, Ph.D.**, is a retired mathematics professor who took up an interest in poetry following his retirement. He enjoys participating in open mics and writing poetry. He is a member of Friends of William Stafford, the Molalla Writers Group, and The Silverton Poetry Association. His favorite poet is William Stafford, one of Larry's former professors at Lewis and Clark College.

**Glen Bledsoe** made his first comic in elementary school and has published over seventeen fiction and non-fiction books since. Comic works include a series for *Salem-News.com,* the graphic novel *The Truant Officer,* and currently a bi-monthly strip for *Ripperologist* magazine called "The Truth." Glen is a middle school art teacher, current president of the Meterite photography club, and Secretary to Assembly 59 of the Society of American Magicians. He teaches T'ai Chi, but doesn't own a television. He can be contacted at glenbledsoe@mac.com.

**Dani Clifton** resides over the river and through the woods with her family, both tamed and wild. Dani can be reached through her website, www.daniclifton.com, or you can find her on Facebook.

**Carrol Haushalter** When not writing or entertaining children in her cowgirl regalia, Carrol can be found on a small farm in Mulino, Oregon with her husband, goats, chickens, and a dog. Her creativity is inspired by the rural environment of her truly western community. Carrol is the author of two western children's books, *Trail From Yesterday* and *Trail to Tomorrow.* The third book of this trilogy, *Trail's End,* is coming soon. Contact her by e-mail at carrolhaushalter@yahoo.com, or at www.thewritecowgirl.blogspot.com.

**Angie Hughes** is the co-founder and director of Portland World Theatre and has participated in over fifty productions in the past twenty years. Some of her writing credits include play adaptations of Japanese ghost stories, three poems with the *Clackamas Literary Review,* and monthly contributions to *Yahoo! Voices.* Her son, Avery, and her husband, Ryan, continue to be her most valued inspiration. Angie's résumé and contact information can be found at www.portlandwt.com.

**Lizzy Welle OeDell** grew up in the country outside of Beavercreek, Oregon. She has always been a writer, starting at a young age, penning the true-life stories of adventures in the woods and escapades held with her best friends. After graduating from Molalla High School, she studied English and writing at Portland State University in Portland, Oregon. Lizzy is a HUGE dog lover, outdoor enthusiast, and Oregon history buff! Contact her at lizzy.o@live.com.

**Pattie PalmerBaker's** art is a partnership between poetry and the book arts, calligraphy and paste paper. Since poetry inspires the image and appears somewhere in the finished collage, it could be said that words are her first love. Whether she is writing a poem or creating an artwork springing from her poetry, she is a translator of the inner world into media the reader or viewer will understand and perhaps be moved by. She can be contacted through her website, www.pattiepalmerbaker.com, or by e-mail at wpbear3311@aol.com.

**K.D. Schmidt** honed her ability to write her compelling memoir through many years in the newspaper industry. Although she has garnered awards for her advertising abilities, this is the first time she has contributed her work to a writing anthology. She is currently working on a novel and enjoys writing poetry. Other interests include photography, Celtic harp playing, and studying Gaelic.

**Devon Seale** has been a short story fantasy writer for several years. He is currently working on his first novel, based on a world he developed during imaginary games played with his younger brother. The chance to be published in *Analekta* has proven to be most exciting for him; the next step in his development as a writer. If you wish to contact him concerning this or other works, please e-mail him at dseale356@gmail.com.

**John Sibley Williams** is the author of *Controlled Hallucinations* (forthcoming, FutureCycle Press) and six poetry chapbooks. He is the winner of the HEART Poetry Award, and finalist for the Pushcart, Rumi, and The Pinch Poetry Prizes. John serves as editor of *The Inflectionist Review*, co-director of the Walt Whitman 150 project, and Book Marketing

Manager at Inkwater Press. A few previous publishing credits include: *Third Coast*, *Inkwell*, *Bryant Literary Review*, *Cream City Review*, *The Chaffin Journal*, *The Evansville Review*, *RHINO*, and various anthologies. His website is johnsibleywilliams.wordpress.com.

## Interior/Cover Designer

**Olivia Croom** is a graphic designer/social media enthusiast from Albuquerque, New Mexico. She made her way to Portland via Ohio and Washington. She graduated from Eastern Washington University and went on to receive her Master's in Book Publishing from Portland State University. She's worked with numerous Portland-area organizations including Hawthorne Books, Literary Arts, Small Doggies Press, and the Oregon Writers Colony. Visit oliviacroom.wix.com/publishing for samples of her work, or email croombooks@gmail.com.

## Co-founders/Editors

**L. Lee Shaw** is the owner of the independent publishing house, Boho Books. Through Boho, she has published two novels, *Blood Will Tell...* and *Monster Child*. She has also facilitated the publication of nine other novels, a poetry chapbook, short stories and a prior anthology, *Mo'Allie*. Shaw has also taught fiction writing, formed a long-running writer's group, hosted a regional writer's conference and had two plays produced and performed. For more information, go to www.bohobooks.com.

**Heather Frazier** works as a freelance editor, helping authors of all genres to polish and perfect their written works. She received both her BA in Arts and Letters and her MA in Book Publishing and Writing from Portland State University in Portland, Oregon. She lives in Molalla, Oregon with her amazing husband, three talented teenagers, two lazy dogs, two crazy cats, and many fish. For more information, contact her via e-mail at editorfrazier@molalla.net, or look her up at www.bohobooks.com.

# Our Thanks

A huge shout-out and thank you to my co-editor, Heather Frazier! Her energy, enthusiasm, and editing skills were the fuel that lifted Analekta off the launch pad. Book designer Olivia Croom mixed her talent and skills, sprinkling the resulting magic on every page. Thank you Olivia for making us look so good! Without a gifted band of writers to fill its pages, Analekta would not exist. An amazingly diverse group, the writers featured herein have collectively set the bar high for future issues. Thank you, each and every one!

—L. Lee Shaw

Thank you, L. Lee Shaw, for making Analekta possible, and believing so strongly in our ability to make this little dream a reality. Much thanks to Vinnie Kinsella for introducing Lee and I, and for having the foresight to figure that we could work well together. I will forever worship Olivia Croom for both her forthright honesty when Lee or I suggested something ridiculous, and her mad skills as a designer. Huge thanks to my awesome little family, Todd, Christen, Devin, and Makayla; they are the best and most loving support system a wife/mom/editor could hope to have. Finally, thank you to all our exceptional contributors; you are the reason Analekta came to be. Loads and loads of love to you all.

—Heather Frazier

# Analekta Submission Guidelines

Submission period for spring edition: opens yearly September 1st, closes December 15th. Submission period for fall edition: opens yearly May 1st, closes August 15th.

Contributors need to reside within Clackamas, Marion, Multnomah, or Washington County to be eligible for publication in this anthology.

We welcome all forms of writing for consideration: Fiction; creative nonfiction; poetry; genre fiction novel excerpts; et cetera.

We invite authors to submit works done in the following genres:

| | |
|---|---|
| Action/Adventure | Humor |
| Chick Lit | Military and Espionage |
| Contemporary | Multicultural |
| Crime | Mystery |
| Fantasy | Offbeat or Quirky |
| Family Saga | Romance |
| Gay and Lesbian | Science Fiction |
| Historical | Thrillers/Suspense |
| Horror | Westerns |

We do not publish genre works of:

| | |
|---|---|
| Children's stories | Religious |
| Children's poetry | Erotica |
| Young Adult | Dark fantasy |

We accept both hardcopy and digital submissions for consideration. Both hardcopy and digital submissions should be formatted in a Microsoft Word document with 1" margins; the document should be set in a 12-point Times New Roman, Cambria, or Ariel font; the document should have numbered pages. The author's name, physical address, e-mail address, phone number, genre and/or form of writing being submitted, and the title of the work should be included on page one of the submission. For example:

Joan Smock
1127 Bellvue DR
Molalla, OR 97038
smock@gmail.com
(503) 555-5555
Fantasy Fiction piece
*Fairyland Adventure*

Hardcopy submissions should include an SASE and be sent to: Boho Books 36179 S Sawtell RD, Molalla, OR 97038.

Digital submissions should be e-mailed to: analekta.molalla@gmail.com.

Minimum acceptable story length is 500 words; maximum length is 3,000 words.

We do accept works that have been submitted to other publications simultaneously, but ask that authors inform us upon submission if this is the case. We also ask for authors to notify us if their work has been accepted for publication elsewhere so that we may withdraw that submission from our selection process.

Upon acceptance for publication in *Analekta*, authors retain all rights to their works published therein.

Please send only one short story, up to four poems, or one creative nonfiction essay per submission.

Authors included in *Analekta* will receive 1 free contributor's copy upon publication.

For more information about *Analekta*, please email L. Lee Shaw or Heather Frazier at analekta.molalla@gmail.com, or find us on Facebook at http://www.facebook.com/analekta.anthology.

CPSIA information can be obtained at www.ICGtesting.com
Printed in the USA
BVOW031637280513

321805BV00001B/20/P